When Love becomes Still-Life

Paul Brookman

Paul Brookman

Introduction

Sill-life, comforted by words, and faith creates a beautiful sadness.

I give you this book.

WHEN LOVE
BECOMES
STILL-LIFE
PAUL BROOKMAN
Poems & Short Stories

Dedicated to Todd, Scotty, Reed, Sharon, Mary, Nathan, Emmy, Connor, and Kaitlynn.

Contents

Morning Mourning Woodpecker

This morning a redheaded woodpecker, pounding on a dead tree pulled my eyelashes from my eyelids. I stared at the ceiling listening to dead bark raining down on the side of the house from each heavy thump. Actually it was nice to be awakened by life. I remember a distant world where most mornings I awoke to the noise of kids fighting and a wife who brought my coffee and would say; "Wake up little biscuit."

I would never wake up to that world again. Through all the chaos and fast movements out the door and in the door after working all day during those times, I am left with this chipping into dead bark.

Sure, I can pinpoint the exact time life changed. The kids were grown and started their own life. My wife and I were headed toward security and retirement with all our insurance policies, 401K, and even though the white picket fence needed paint, life had all the quietness of a small town. My wife was diagnosed with MDS,(*Myelodysplastic Syndrome*), a form of Leukemia, or a type of cancer in which the bone morrow does not make enough healthy blood cells and there are abnormal (blast) cells in the blood and/or bone marrow. She became transfusion dependent and time was running out. The body can only handle so many transfusions. The doctors said about thirty-five. The same amount of chips into dead bark that woodpecker is making every minute.

The pounding and the thumping continued. Each day when my eyelashes separated from my eyelids, I wanted to close them again. I had a hard time watching life being taken from her, and counting each transfusion; temporarily making her perk up for a week, only to bring lethargy and bone pain the next. No one, not the kids who were now adults, her sister or brother, or my family could know what level of hell we were in, and maybe only Dante understood because he described a place in hell for lovers, losing everything, and paying the price for our own folly, believing love can conquer all.

There was hope. A bone marrow transplant. The doctors at *John Hopkins* said my fiercely independent wife, once the transplant was done, within a month, would return to her occupation as an Accountant and resume a normal life bringing me coffee again and saying; "Wake up little biscuit." Everyone was in agreement except me. I am a cynic when something sounds too good to be true. In this situation there really was no way I could not go along with it, especially when the call came that a 100% match had been found.

They readied her for the transplant and killed everything in her body with chemo. The bone marrow was flown from Tennessee to Baltimore. They released her to me a couple weeks later. On the night of her released, she developed a severe headache. Calling an ambulance was not an option because only Hopkins could deal with her condition, so from my home in Annapolis, I sped her to Baltimore, in the snow, and got there in amazing time.

She had a brain bleed in her Occipital Lobe. A spot about

the size of a nickel in her brain that is now just grey matter and dead. Calling the youngest son, my voice stuttered. I'm sure he didn't like receiving information from me, because I struggled with saying bad news. Try telling a mother's son that she is now blind. Try and get the words out of your throat and move your hyoid and say your wife is now blind when you know how important her sight is for her occupation, driving, and her independence in life without getting choked up.

Everything was slow and agonizing. The horror continued and kept getting worse. A beautiful and sexy redhead, now bald, blind and seventy-eight pounds. Two intestinal infections making her stomach the size of a basketball, all because her body lost resistance. The brain trauma that left her with rare hallucinatory seizures and incredible fear. Several times walking in on "code blue" being called on your wife. It wasn't long before that white picket fence fell down around us.

This was just the beginning. I don't think anyone will ever understand what happened to us in the next two years. To this day my voice still stutters and my eyes well-up just talking about it. I can barely write about it, and I really don't want to write about it.

But this morning I blame that redheaded woodpecker pounding on that dead tree, and dried bark sounding against this empty house, pulling my eyelashes from my eyelids. It reminds me of her and what she was always able to awaken and bring out of my heart. It is my morning, my mourning, my own made coffee, remembering her voice; "Wake up little biscuit."

Instead of taking a shotgun to the woodpecker, I completed this book.

When Love Becomes Still-Life

Nothing is louder than a heart unforgiven,
Screaming in the afternoon
Among an oil colored room of flowers and drapes
While loneliness distills sunlight into a white
paste.
Without wind to move petals or linens
Or of reaching hands across a wooden table
Toward a bowl of red apples without taste.
The serpent is through with me
No footsteps arriving or heels departing
Just the meter noise of a reckless beat
When love becomes still-life,
Long after Cézanne left the kitchen,
Nothing is louder than a heart unforgiven.

Even a condemned man has a priest
Saying prayers, walking together,
An electric chair would feel like life.
Forgiveness, relief for soul, not heart,

An electric hum drowns the noise of each beat.
Far better than this still-life grief
Shouting from this squalor canvass
Downsized and ripped apart
As the rich sun begins to depart.

You confess to the night,
Curse the moon, picked fruit
And the world that does not think twice,
Causing havoc among the stars
Shattering ceramic bowls into jagged pieces.

Hear the awkward rolling of red apples
Thumping off our wooden table
Falling from Paradise
When love becomes still-life.
Nothing is louder than a heart unforgiven.
You let go,
And allow Van Gogh into your kitchen.

Grief

Forever reaching,
Playing tag
With a butterfly.

Third Week Of Every July

Those times taking the children to the shore
Vacationing from work
All the buildings in a city
And lack of horizons there.
Our lives were deep breaths on a strong pier.
We held that breath
Till the next year.
How you saved shells and placed them in tissue,
Only for us to discover them again in bleak
November
Adding strength, to make it till the next summer.
In waves coming to shore
I watched you die many times
Until it became normal as morning coffee.
I watched you saving the shells
Filling a tissue with something other than tears.
I could not stop the fluid that sadness creates.
The kind of fluid splashing against a pier.

*Those moments of a sound sucking the entire
ocean
Back into the horizon,
And what swept through our lives.
Amusements and taffy shops on the boardwalk.
Flipping quarters to the children to use on the
machines of lights,
While sunburned skin chilled us in those walks at
night.
Waves kept coming, they always do.
Some bigger than others.
The morning coffee I made,
Rubbing my forehead
Above the cup's aroma.
Is this the wave that will suck me into the horizon?
What's left of the shoddy piers?
The machine lights long ago disappeared
Among blinding sparkles of upturned empty sand
Where only seagulls are left to circle and scream.
Another summer's mirth returns
With human voices among the surf,
Blankets, towels, and chairs arrive
And applied coconut lotion mixes with the salt air.
We will always be there
Long after the taking of the piers,
You and your long flowing hair
Being tied above your shoulders,
Somewhere on the horizon
Even in bleak November
When tissues fill with something other than tears.*

PLAYLAND

Time to Go

Conforming waves hissing further
  along cool sand
Foaming last words along the beach
Pick up the last shell and take
  my hand
Gone are the scents of coconut lotions
Roasted skin and salty sweat
  licked lips
Kissed when love seemed endless
Gone are the screams of seagulls
  feeding on
Boardwalk fries and Cheese Curls
Few remain walking along the
  water line
Behind the hissing, foaming last
  words
"Time to go."
Carnival hucksters packing up,
  retreating to Florida

Iron shutters pulled down, locked on
    Pizza By The Slice,
Frozen dipped cones and flavored ice.
Pick up the last shell and take
    my hand
To a place where falling leaves replace
    the sand
Please my beloved make it through
    December
Make it to May
And fear not our time to go.

Autumn

I love fall,
Falling in love
As leaves fall
Lyrically sweetly swooning
On a crisp night
Under a blue moon.
A heart of darker reds
And orange hues
Transfuse us all.

Notice me before winter.
Before the wind is screaming
Through trees without leaves
At this last moment of awe.

Still-Harmony

A Cardinal is the last one at the
    feeder.
The rising moon, hiding it's face
In and out of a cloud or shroud.
Wind embracing a light rain,
Dancing without stars
Everything comes and goes,
Enduring while the cat is sleeping.

Church Circle

Traffic lights absolving pedestrians' haste
Genuflecting off curbs
Against the red and green commands.
Doing penance for their pace
Unaware of a descending October evening
Darkening red bricks
Littered with damp leaves
Causing tires and feet to slip.
Workdays always surrender
Some to a chilled wind whipping around the circle,
Powerful enough to be a new task master
Issuing demotions of sniffles
For forgetting a coat,
At times, gentle enough
To be lazy with a sweater.

Racing to their parking spots
Entering streets crawling to a wider sprawl,
The church in the circle's womb

Birth the sound of bells through alleyways.
Saint Anne's motherly voice
Tolls for the lonely and unwed,
Ringing as a leaf falls.

No one notices the girl in her office.
No notice of her at all
Bathed in a golden light.
A host raised above after six o'clock
Her window a chalice
Within a red brick tabernacle,
No notice of her or Annapolis at twilight
Or even of the bells that rang minutes ago,
Forgotten,
Might as well been some October evening three
hundred years or so,
Same colors, red bricks, and the human feet
that slip
On the damp leaves.

Or of someone like me under a streetlamp now lit
A moment among the movement,
Long enough to see her put on a sweater
And her forearms become relics in the sleeves.
Turning off the light, emerging in the twilight,
Entering the weather
And then the church in the circle's womb
Perhaps to pray for a man
Who writes these words on wafer for her to
consume.

Annapolis Streets

Church Circle,
This town's marquee
Ringing bells of 300 hundred years
Opens a curtain,
Two shows a night
Coming and going
Ghosts get in free.

Going at midnight
Aging in my walking
Limping red brick to red brick
Toward the Circle's womb.
An audience of ghosts arrive
Wind flirting with leaves
Shuffling to their seats
Guided by prisms of footlights
Caused by wet streets.

One line of poetry

To this audience of the night
Satisfies them as I take flight
Hearing their applauding rain
And breathing wind.
Exiting into Rams Head's alley
Avoiding autograph dwellers
Seeking spare change and cigarettes.

Looking back toward West Street,
Noticing a cute brunette
Limping toward the Circle
Wondering
What the ghosts' demand of her.

Gerald Fischman Rob Hiaasen John McNamara Rebecca Smith Wendi Winters

5 shot dead
At The Capital

Stationary Sailboats

On my way home in Annapolis tonight
There is less traffic
Like the small town
We used to be.

A stillness on the bay without wind.
Stationary sailboats,
A pained quietness.

How an evil deed
Pauses us to take a breath
Of being alive,
As we exhale sorrow for the five
Not going home tonight.

Guide-Dog

A guide-dog's life is hell,
Far more than the blind
Holding the leash.

Annapolis Shallows

Inside her room where bodies spent
On a sweat-stained couch marking days
With voices raised and a window where love went.
How she wanted iambic pentameter
A drinking song to sing upon the Chesapeake.
Annapolis has moved on, so has she
From love so wrong toward money in these ports.

Annapolitan boats and clothing
Blue blazers or salmon shorts
Sailing toward their ego-alley mooring,
Becoming pedestrian up Main Street to her place.
Docking on hard wooden flooring
Adapting an easy embrace on nights
Without a crescent moon or iambic pentameter
In her room near the window where her ex went.

Annapolis men and ladies spent adrift
In the Bay's shallows, limbo ledges to Hades.

Sipping Sauvignon Blanc, leaving half-drunk glasses
Of this unnamed varietal next to empty beach chairs
On private piers and walking planks
In front of houses with long ascending stairs.

Mutiny moves her
Stealing bounty of breadfruit
Setting ship ablaze.
Her Pitcairn Island is not heaven
But shallows, ledges to Hades
Blowing stout midshipmen to hunchbacks
Dominating yacht club members with a titanic whip
A storm's unrelenting slapping of a boat against slip.

Her turbulent wake of her escaping
Downstream of her solid body moving through shallows
One last mutiny for what her only love ignored.
No notice of her from the wealthy shoreline
No answer to the knocking on her door
At apartment number nine.

Wind

Wind,
Prankster of October leaves
Swirling under a magician's wand
Taking from branches and limbs
That once reached out in the summer sun
Full of dreams, and enclosing our days
When love was young.

Limbs picked by chilling breezes
Throwing yellow and orange to the ground.
The vanity of love scratching the streets,
Moving around, at times lingering,
At times dying in the wetness of the gutter.

Wind,
Prankster of October leaves
Bending egos that rise above
Greeting the sun with flutter.

Vibrant veins that once gave flesh to sky
Now fall in gusts of folly,
Autumn tears of sumner's lies.

When Love Tastes Like Paste

When love tastes like paste,
Glue that once held us together
Is absent a forgiving flavor
Or embrace of sweet or sour.
"I love you;"
Texted apart during a light rain
Outside my window where children
Just sat drawing on the driveway pavement
Some innocent hearts with arrows
Before moving children indoors
Before the sidewalk chalk
Is bleeding edges of green grass
To pale, dull blades.

Sort of misreading and misleading
A tapered neighborhood lawn
Only for consecrating a past with meaning,
Some childish scribbling
Now milking

Pooling along the edging.

Love is an action word
Upon word upon word
Till book or poem is finished
And bound so human hands can hold
The strength or weakness of heart and soul.

But here we are
In such an unbinding state,
Over and over again
Writing with chalk
On concrete slabs
Where wind cannot turn pages
And rain falling with an erase
When love tastes like paste.

Last Thing To Go

Where kisses go that's been kissed,
All kisses ever kissed?
A list of things pressed to my lips,
Foreheads, cheeks, inner thighs,
Bourbon or the sweeter sister rye.
There must be an immortal trace
Of kissing,
Like judgement for my sins when I die.
Lovers left without last rites
Or crucified,
Read my sins with those lips I've kissed.
I kissed you well,
Earned my place for lovers in Dante's hell.

Lift up these weights on my face,
Cheeks of foreskin cover my chin.
Read my sins,
The immortal trace;
You swirled her lipstick on her face,

Made a Pollack painting with your tongue.

Where have all the kisses gone?
Pour morphine over my crusted lips
Till all that's left of me is hearing
Harsh sparks of a cold October rain
On crisp leaves.
Now I recall without a list
I was never forgiven with a kiss.

Natatorial

Children laugh at the wonder
When they discover
Some birds swim.

Flake Of Snow

I once
Was a flake of snow.
Fell a mile or so
Down
As wintery wind began blowing,
Sighing
Between houses dusting white
And trees wearing wedding gowns
At midnight.

Down
Farther than roof tops,
Swirling around
Above the parking lots below
And rising again
Not knowing where to go
In this mid-air break.

To now be a fragile star shape

And so unnoticed in my pain.

I want to drop like rain,
Escape
From this great height,
But I am snow
And what heaven has iced.

Who is awake
To see this falling
Flake,
To see this blur
Among them all?
Who is there to break my fall?
I once
Was a flake of snow
Fell a mile or so
Onto the tongue of a child I melted slow.

Going Out

He softens his stash with conditioner
In case his lips are kissed.
Chews mint gum for breath
In case his tongue is met.
Deodorizes, adds a scent with cologne,
Presses clothes,
And straightens the home to show no mess.

The music and the moon is hung
In the air around his flight.
But one thing he left a mess
In search of worthiness this night
And his desire to be kissed;
His sloppy, unorganized broken heart
Cause only one can groom what he missed.

She Drove A Ford

All her belongings piled to the back window.
Obstructing past visions of her abandoned sons in
the rear view mirror.
Her flea market on wheels, ready for unloading at
the next man's place.
The many men she took up with, always ended the
same;
With payment of a hotel bill, or an empty driveway
to park awhile.
The many holes in walls left behind, from bashing
heads,
Or poundings fists.
She left for others to plaster the walls in her now
vacated rooms.
Because they let love start an engine.

Her emotions were a road hazard.
The dump truck and turning barrel of mortar

Even as the windshield took stones, and chips of
concrete,
You thought you could maneuver.
We are all lonesome on our journey,
Give her comfort in the passenger seat,
Driving intoxicated.
But drivers are replaceable at her next rest stop.
Those roadside tables selling used goods,
Litter the windows panes speeding on the highway.

After she had sucked the air out, the tires are
refilled.
The windshield is replaced and vision unimpaired.
Her smile was a pothole that cannot be filled,
Never any tar of caring once through with her ride.

It goes on.

She gets behind the wheel of her Ford.
Belongings piled to the back window,
Glancing the rearview mirror, seeing her sons,
Until ghosts mingled with dust raised acceleration,
And a radio country song
Drowns the voices she hears calling, "mom."

Sometimes Twilight Does Not Appear

Sometimes twilight does not appear.
Moments before dawn or after sunset
It does not show,
Does not relieve hope or despair
Before or after Earth's longer spin is met.
It does not glow a soul's blue light
Before night is marrow black
Or day is bone white.
Clouds hide enough to turn all gray
Without goodbye
To prelude a long day, or lullaby night.
Thus hope or despair is endless
When Earth's longer spin is without twilight.

The Cove

A winter brook flows to
Warmer, muddier waters. What we call
Love, eternal babbling over stones,
Flushing into spaces of courts and divisions
Around the bay. A body handles
Only so many transfusions,
And each heart becomes unforgiving.
Love, greedy Leukemia, and lethargic,
Everything good must first be killed
To ready the marrow for transplant.

Where love once cast at first sight,
Blood bleeds into the occipital lobe

And blinds the dreams that bind,
Flushing into spaces of courts and divisions
Around the mind. He has signed
The DO NOT RESUSCITATE Order,
And blood became thicker than water.

Day Without Demands

Saturday of no demands.
A day like every day
More of the same, less of the same.
Newspaper pages turning
As the Sun cast shadows through the French door
pane.
All kindle for the coming burning
On a day beginning without demands.

We found ourselves in the morning leisure
Till a fearful stare
Trembling of hands
And the beginning of a seizure.
One hand held the arm at the elbow
And lifted the hand on fire.

Felt like a liar for I saw and smelled nothing.
Could not extinguish the flame
Nor soothe her words

Or her scream of pain
Expelled through the frothing.

Hallucinations came with our tea,
My flesh peeled from face to bone.
Because once the brain bleeds
The demon breaks into the home
During morning leisure
Or peaceful night,
Where love once cast at first sight
Now rapes my wife with seizure.

She will remember nothing of my valor.
Nothing of my voice
Lost among the noise.
Or of me fighting off the rapist
Or the slashing and cutting of my hyoid.
Just my hand that delivered the Ativan
To resume the day without demands.

ST. ELIZABETHS

St. Elizabeth's Bus Stop Lament

Tried for treason
Declared insane,
But how many of us left love
As a dangling participle exiled
From the United States?
A headline read:
"US POET FOUND DEAD"
And in his death was claimed.

Bikers

Bikers are all the same,
Dress alike, not really tough
When fearing rain.
Their women,
Heartsick and rough,
Breasts of better days
Hold on to their man.
Freedom is just an exhaust
When believing
Riding is enough.
Sometimes
You have to lay the bike down
Choose what to bruise,
And see what survives the gravel ground.

9203

The Last Delivery

His hand was shaking putting the last pieces of mail in the box for the residence just off West Street in Annapolis. A few plastic trays of mail pick-ups were left to take back to the station. This was James Finamore's last day, officially retiring as an employee of the Annapolis Post Office after thirty-eight years.

He still had one last delivery.

Over the years, he routinely showed up at Annapolis Middle School, picking up his granddaughter after work in his 2010 Hyundai Sonata.

Caroline was a month away from graduating and going into high school. After classes she walked to Pop-Pop's old Hyundai, oblivious, and texting her girlfriends and boyfriends. She would say; "Hi Pop-Pop," resuming her texting while he always delivered her safely to his son's house.

The Hyundai wasn't there and she saw him waiting in the Post office jeep. She saw there wasn't a passenger seat and he told her to just hop in and sit behind the few trays of mail due back at the station, and now thirty minutes late.

"Did your car breakdown Pop-Pop?"

"No Caroline, I just wanted to show and tell you something on my last day as a mailman."

He drove to a cul-de-sac on his route and said; "No one waits for the mailman anymore. Even dogs no longer bark or chase the mailman. My world is obsolete Caroline, and though somethings are gone, it is important for me to share this with you today."

He told her how he used to deliver cards and love letters, and could tell by the outside envelopes the affections people were showing to one another and how love is now emailed.

"In my day, men and women were once judged and seen through their handwriting, but now are measured by typed texts. Spell-Check now corrects errors. "Send" is pressed to deliver a message. Everything is bulk mail advertising or packages from Amazon. No one waits by the curb."

"Only your Grandma, and some like her are left doing such things. Maybe you and other kids will notice their elderly scrawl of sending their love, and experience an occasional postal rejoice of, "Look what I got in the mail from Nanny!"

"When I was a boy we were all enticed by the comic book ads, and would send away for X-RAY SPECS looking for a super human vision upon the world, or Sea Monkeys, and small, live Seahorses. We would wait at the curb for the mailman every day till those things arrived. That excitement is long gone. The world grew more sophisticated, artificially smart, and the magic of Sea Monkeys became just brine shrimp."

"I wanted to tell you Caroline, don't marry a man till you see his handwriting. Don't marry a man who will not wait by the curb for you. Find a man who believes in Sea Monkeys, sends you love letters in the mail, and wants X-RAY SPECS."

James Finamore delivered Caroline home, returned the jeep and retired.

The Saloonkeeper's Son
Temptation Eyes

My teenage hormones were out of control. Every day I saw my brother Larry come and go in his new, mean-green AMC Javelin. A 343 cubic –inch, four-barrel V8, 280 horsepower machine that went from zero-to-sixty in less than seven seconds.

I just turned fifteen, a freshman in high school and Larry a freshman in college. I wanted the freedom to jump into the black bucket seat, and ride my dreams into the night. A little piece of that freedom machine and of an older girl named Karen with mean-green eyes. Two things I wanted and too young to pursue. In my madness to control myself, I would impute the pain of my unrequited loves by listening to the Grassroots new song; "Temptation Eyes," till one day an opportunity presented itself, and I snapped.

Larry was going to a party with his guy friends and wasn't taking his Javelin. He left the keys for me to stare at while the 45 record of "Temptation

Eyes" played over and over. That arm would reach the end of the record, scratch a couple times, and move back to the beginning to play the song again as phonographs did in those days.

Madness for mean-green eyes, and a mean-green machine made the temptation too great to stop my impulse. I was about to become a criminal, steal my brother's car, drive without a license, and pursue a girl I wanted a chance to be near. Who thinks of consequences when raging hormones makes you stupid?

I grabbed the keys, unlocked the door and slipped into the softest leather I had ever felt in my life. I turned the ignition switch and heard a purr like the biggest lion in the jungle. I knew Larry had an 8 track tape of the grassroots and into the slot it went and headed to Karen's house.

Thought about how when she saw me, she would run in her red floral hippy dress and jump into the other bucket seat. With "Temptation Eyes" playing in the background, her long, flowing hair whipping around in the car cruising down Pennsylvania Avenue Extended as we reached the speed of light that would make our time together stand still.

I was urged to notice the sluggishness but ignored it. I was having too much fun. A car load of older, teenage babes waved and smiled at me. What a chic-magnet I had become! Even the Maryland State Trooper passed me without trouble, so everything was going well.

The sun was going down as I pulled in front of Karen's house. I knocked at the door confident and cocky, and when she answered I said; "Hi, just came over to take you for a ride."

"Paul, you are in the 9th grade and I know you don't have a license or a car," she said walking off her porch toward the Javelin.

"Whose car is this?"

"It's OURS for the night;" I said, as best a fifteen year old could romantically utter. I was a smooth talker and just making an assumptive close.

"What's that burning smell ?" Pausing briefly with her cute upturned nostrils snorting the air

"You idiot, you're driving with the emergency brake on!"

I watched the back of that red, floral hippy dress return to her front door as she muttered her love for me; "Look kid, you dumb ass, take that car back and go home."

Feeling like an ashamed child who just pissed the bed, I headed home.

I found and released the emergency brake and headed down Marlboro Pike to the Dixie Pig, and sat in the car eating four pork bar-b-cue sandwiches. I gathered my wits and stopped at the gas station and filled the tank so my brother wouldn't notice and by ten in the evening pulled back into the driveway of my house.

What I didn't know was Joe, my best friend in the neighborhood was frantically looking for me. Those hot babes who waved at me early on were headed to the same party my brother was at, and told Larry and his buddies they didn't know I had a license. Joe couldn't get to me before I entered the house, but once I did, and saw all the furniture moved from the living room to the dining room to create a boxing ring, I knew I was about to get my ass beat.

My brother Larry was more than angry. He was savage angry.

My adventure had gone from just pissing the bed, to fully shitting the bed. I didn't even bother to raise my hands and protect myself. I was wrong. I let Larry vent his words and punch my face. The night of "Temptation Eyes" ended with two black eyes and swollen cheeks.

I would do it all again. To be fifteen, and drive that mean-green Javelin to pursue a girl with mean-green eyes. Who wouldn't? Only the next time, I would do it with the emergency brake off.

The Saloonkeeper's Son
First Confession

Marlboro Pike stretches in both directions in front of the church, bending westward to places in District Heights like The Shady Oak Inn, where many fathers stopped for a drink before coming home after work, or The Mighty Mo car hop restaurant where an Orange Freeze and a Teen Twist sandwich were served on a tray that hooked to a car's window. A small shopping center, stores like Drug Fair where you could get a fountain cherry Coke and a Superman comic book, Giant Grocery store, a beauty parlor, or across the street to a shopping strip with Clark's music store, Gallo's or Eddie Leonard's sandwich shop and a gas station, and further along the Pike a firehouse, and a Tasty Freeze.

Eastward from the church, Marlboro Pike went into Forestville to places in the Penn Mar Shopping Center like the Horn and Horn Restaurant,

Peoples Drug Store, Thom McCan Shoes and Woolworths.

Along both routes, small medical services of all kinds.

No train tracks, just houses and houses in the new suburbs of Washington D.C. taking shape in this new era of development and flight from the City. The paper boys worked many hours delivering The Washington Evening Star, The Washington Post, and my favorite, The Washington Daily News. Television Stations were growing from four, to five, and if the antenna on the roof was pointed correctly, a Baltimore channel was possible.

Mount Calvary Church was meant to grow with the Catholic community that lived in the look-a-like houses coming out of the fifties and into the early sixties. The families began to attend funerals, baptisms, weddings, Sunday services, communions and confessions in the new church while their children were attending the Catholic grade school.

Teenagers hung out and some created gangs in their rebellion of a place that was full of rules, rituals, and boredom. Some joined The Catholic Teen Club, joined bowling leagues, and played sports.

At that time, the age of seven, making your first confession as a Catholic was a requirement before making your first communion. Since my first day of Catholic school at the age of six, I was told what was right or wrong by a brutal gang of nuns in black habits who referred to me as; "The saloon keeper's son." I was smacked the first day of school for putting my lunch bag in the wrong place. These were the days before air conditioning or cold packs, and these nuns did everything possible to keep the smell of four hour old tuna fish sandwiches from permeating the air in the hot, humid, beginning of the school year. But I had till the "age of reason," before I had to worry about confessing my new understanding of sins and salmonella poisoning.

During the ages of six and seven, the nun's power would enter my mind. Sometimes while playing in my parent's tavern, I would use the miniature bottles of alcohol as toy soldiers. Jim Beam would crush the onslaught of Seagram's 7, Seagram's Gin, and Seagram's VO every time, until a nun's voice would enter my mind that alcohol is evil. So in the next battle I would let the mighty giant Ketchup win against Jim Beam with the help of salt and pepper shakers. The cost was high on the battle field of the table when the cap of Ketchup loosened, leaving a bloody mess. War is ugly.

Concepts of right or wrong in playing war was easy, but sex and the feelings I was having was not as easy. Yes, Mighty Mouse's girlfriend turned me on. Even when Bugs Bunny went drag in a few cartoons I got a tingle. I was sure it was a sin because of the reaction the nuns had when dragging poor Cecil Webb out of the boy's bathroom for touching himself while looking at Veronica in an Archie comic book.

Cecil had figured out during our coming "age

of reason" that it was a sin to touch yourself, so he moved on to devising ways to get girls to touch him. He had cut a hole in his baggy pant's pocket and then asked a girl to get his milk money while acting like his hands were too busy holding papers and school books. Her scream brought the attention of the nuns and poor Cecil was whipped, and sent packing to public school. Cecil actually became a successful fashion designer and designed Parachute Pants for MC Hammer in the early 80's.

Easter was approaching. It was time for my first confession. The entire class was led into that big church next door, no talking, and none of us were joking around. I felt like James Cagney in the movie "Angels With Dirty Faces" being escorted to the electric chair. Each nun had a metal clicker in their hand, directing us without speaking. We took our places in the pews, and I was glad I was not in the front row so I had time to think what to say before entering one of the boxes lining the sides of the church.

The old Monsignor sat in a chair at the Alter. A double click echoed in that silent church and the first group of kids were being directed to make their confession to him, in full view of others in the church. He was hard of hearing, so his voice began echoing the punishments he was dealing out. Behind him and the alter, that enormous, life-like crucifixion scene was a horror to view by a little boy in a pew trying to think what I had done and what will be my punishment. I began wishing I was the Roman soldier holding that long spear. I wanted to lance the nuns, swing it wildly to avoid capture and make my escape out the church.

I didn't want the nun to point our pew toward the old Monsignor, but the dark boxes wasn't much of an option either. The clicks kept sounding and time was running out for me.

"Click, click." The nun stood at our pew and pointed out what place we were to go. I got a box, and waited behind a couple of boys. The small light atop the box turned green and the boy in front of me entered, and then a light turned to red. How did that happen? Who knew that half of the box was taken? On the other side of the box the light went green and out came a kid and another went in. I knew my time had come.

The red light went off and the green light went on. Jeff Will came out and held the curtain open for me so that he could whisper something to me.

"You are going to hell Brookman."

Not what I wanted to hear.

I walked in and could hardly see, but knelt on a loose, hard cushioned stoop in front of the darkened window pane with small squares and a tiny hole in each center not allowing you to see through, but your voice could be heard by the priest. I quickly figured out the pressure of my kneeling on the loose board was causing the light to change from green to red. I had to memorize for this, and had come up with a sin that I lied to my mother about brushing my teeth. I should get off easy.

A panel was pulled opened and a slight twilight in his area made the priest a shadow. The small squares distorted any recognizing of his face and doubled the size of his head. It was the image I saw looking at me through the window pane of my house door. I had trouble speaking, but no trouble shaking. I'm sure that light was flickering red and green outside the box.

"Are you ready to confess your sins?"

I took a breath and once I began talking I couldn't stop. I was like a criminal trying to tell everything I know to plea bargain a better sentence.

"Bless me father for I have sinned, this is my first confession. I played with myself while looking at Bugs Bunny dressed like a girl. I played with myself while looking at Veronica in an Archie comic book. I never really liked Betty. I was the one who gave the Archie comic book to Cecil, it wasn't even his. I too cut a whole in my pocket and Debbie Butler put her hand in my pocket and she touched me. She didn't scream. She didn't let go and kept smiling."

I didn't know what to do next. Cecil was already sent away and he wasn't there to tell me what to do next and I didn't want to be sent away to the corn field by the nuns.

I saw the movie *Bells of St.Mary's*. I don't like nuns, they are just Ingrid Bergman wannabes, and hate the clickers they carry.

The confessional went silent and seemed like eternity. I was sure that priest was waiting for his head to stop spinning. Then the verdict was rendered; "Say three Hail Mary's and make a good act of contrition."

The Saloonkeeper's Son
The Picture

News spread quickly on the night of Thursday, April 4, 1968. Protests turned into riots in Washington D.C. especially along U Street NW and 14th Street NW. Mayor Walter Washington asked President Lyndon Johnson for help, and Johnson ordered National Guard and federal troops into the city. A citywide curfew was declared at 11:00 p.m.

By Friday the curfew extended everywhere. Businesses shut down. My mother and Father came home from the bar only after Metropolitan Police sergeant walked in, slammed his shotgun on a table, and shouted; "This place is closed. Get out."

I rarely saw my parents home together except on Christmas and even then, lots of the regulars from the bar were celebrating with us. Only three other times had it happened: every four years when the Presidential election closed bars during voting hours; when President Kennedy's funeral shut businesses for an official day of mourning; and once, when a regular at the bar asked a guy if he wanted to play some numbers. Turned out it was an FBI agent having a beer and the tavern's liquor license was suspended for three days. Now, Dr. King's death joined those rare still-life moments.

By Saturday, full-scale riots, arson, looting, and clashes spread across the city. Johnson deployed nearly 12,000 federal troops and 1,750 National Guardsmen - one of the largest domestic troop deployments in U.S. history. Fires burned in neighborhoods, and thousands were arrested for curfew violations.

That night, my father wanted to take a shotguns, and my older brother John to guard the tavern. Couldn't figure out what was worth protecting? Was it cases of bottle neck beers, half used liters of liquor at the bar, or a few pictures, like a large one of John when he was seven years old posing in a fighter's stance with Boxing gloves, shorts, and shoes? I never got my picture taken at seven years old looking like I just beat up a stuffed animal and becoming super lightweight champion of the bedroom. I just didn't think John was interested in protecting it.

John was the smart older brother, a reader who didn't talk much. Among his books I discovered *Nigger: An Autobiography* by comedian Dick Gregory. On the cover, Gregory had written: *"Dear Momma - Wherever you are, if ever you hear the word nigger again, remember they are advertising my book.*"

His humor cut deep truths about racism and segregation. One story stuck with me: Gregory wrote about eating in the South, when two good old boys approached him, while Gregory was holding his knife and fork ready to cut into his chicken dinner. "Anything you do to that chicken boy," they told him, "we're gonna do to you." Gregory picked up the chicken and kissed it.

The tavern itself was a long, narrow shoebox attached to a liquor store, which stood next to Morton's, a large retail shop. When I returned with my mother on her first day back, the liquor store's windows were smashed and spirits looted. Morton's had been gutted. Six huge display windows shattered, mannequins thrown onto the sidewalk, glass glittering among broken limbs. Morton's was where everyone shopped during "Crazy Days" sales: ten pairs of Ban-Lon socks or ten packs of pantyhose for $1.99.

It was odd the tavern hadn't been touched or torched. Maybe it didn't draw a crowd like Morton's or the liquor store. Maybe it was luck or divine intervention. No one could have known my father was inside with his shotgun.

Inside, Mr. Wildcat Wilson was at the first table by the jukebox, ready to greet anyone with, "Happy New Year." He was busy smoking over a horse racing form and sipping iced tea. Genro, a portly, bearded ex-postal worker was at a booth closest to the bar.

At the bar was two bricklayers drinking draft

beers, Norman drinking Chivas and rounding it out toward the kitchen next to the waitress station of cocktail napkins, straws, and matches was Parakeet - a neighborhood eccentric with a bird-like face with a pointed beaklike nose, and an annoying habit of ending conversations asking, "Don't you love me anymore?"

I restocked a case of bottle neck Schlitz for the cold box behind the bar. Parakeet pestered me with questions about the riots which I didn't feel like talking about. Then came the question; "Don't ya love me anymore?"

"Hell no Parakeet. You're touched in the head." The bricklayers got a chuckle out of it.

A young black man, a stranger came in and walked to the back of the bar and sat next to Para-keet. My mother served him a draft and I went and sat in booth and sipped ginger ale.

Everything seemed to be getting back to normal until the young stranger asked Parakeet to pass him a pack of matches from the waitress station.

Parakeet sneered, "Get it yourself, nigger."

I looked toward my mother who was serving Mr Wilson another iced tea and didn't hear it. The bricklayers and Genro did.

The young man said nothing, got up and got his matches and left. The bricklayers and Genro lit into ParaKeet calling him a "stupid shit."

Now my 5 foot tall Italian mother in heals got up to speed, threatening to ban him and telling him this is her place. Twenty minutes later, Genro who had stepped outside, rushed back in.

"They're coming back," he shouted. "The young black fella and a carload of black guys and one has a shotgun."

My mother told me : "Paul, hide Parakeet in the basement."

I tucked him into a hollow in the underground brick walls and stacked beer cases in front of him. By the time I came upstairs, a shotgun was pointed at my mother. The man asked where the man who called his friend a nigger? Calmly, she told him she banned him and threw him out.

He told the young man to go look around and see if he's here and took off into the kitchen toward the basement. I pictured Parakeet saying to these guys, "Don't ya love me," just before being thrown off the Sousa bridge.

He asked my mother as he lowered the shot-gun; "Do you know why your bar wasn't hit in the riots?"

She just slightly shook her head no.

"It was because of that picture," as he points to the back wall near where I was standing. I thought he was talking the large picture of my older brother.

He explained further that it was known in the neighborhood Heavyweight Champion Joe Lewis visited my father in the early 60's at the bar and my mother was always welcoming to everyone.

The young man returned and thankfully he didn't find Parakeet. I was sure Parakeet was going to be thrown off the Sousa Bridge that day and was glad when they left.

Everyone started gathering themselves and

talking fast for the next half hour. There wasn't any need to call the Police. I then went to the basement to get Parakeet. He seemed like a winged bird. My mother banned him and told him not to come back for a month.

I couldn't help thinking that the riots actually had some crowd control to it. When my mother told the story to others the picture of my father with Joe Lewis was the hero in her story.

Genro put a coin in the jukebox and the song; "*I Can't Stop Loving You,*" by Ray Charles began playing.

Parakeet started slowly walking out, ashamed while his bird head slumped in his shoulders.

"Happy New Year!" Mr. Wilson shouted as Parakeet raised his hand to push open the door out the bar.

One of the bricklayers quickly hollered out; "Hey Parakeet, Don't ya love us anymore?"

About the Author

A boxer's most important punch is the jab. It may not end a fight, but it sets up everything that does. It keeps your opponent busy and forces them to play defense. That momentary stun is opportunity. It takes discipline and patience. The jab becomes the setup all other punches follow. But always — *keep your hands up.*

So too for comics and their routines, poets and their poems.

I was a blessed anomaly — given the gift of exposure to all three art forms.

First, as a young boy, My father, a Washington D.C. Golden Gloves Middleweight with a 54–5 amateur record, turned professional at 18. He was known as a hard-punching brawler with a strong chin, but after an impressive 25–5 start, his career floundered. He told me it would've been different had he signed with a big-time (and corrupt) New York promoter.

So what does a boxer do when his career ends and he only has a sixth-grade education? He becomes a bodyguard for a local gangster, saves his money, and opens a tavern in a gritty working-class D.C. neighborhood called Anacostia.

That tavern became my front-row seat to the world — bookmakers, journeymen fighters, title contenders, and even a Heavyweight Champion named Joe Louis. I was just a boy, hanging out in the bar, when someone — maybe even Joe — gave me a playful, quick slap and said, *"Get those hands up."*

My life has been full of jabs. And keeping my hands up.

I remember those fighters' large, remarkably fast hands — and later, how some hands trembled lifting a beer. "He took one too many punches to the head," my father would say.

I spent a lot of time alone growing up and discovered poetry right around the time I discovered girls. I kept it hidden like a Playboy under the mattress. I didn't think the people in the bar — or even my family — would understand. My uncle once called it *"poultry."*

Privately, I trained like a boxer. I devoured books on poetry. My prized possession was the *Princeton Encyclopedia of Poetry and Poetics*. I shadowboxed with free verse, haikus, and sonnets. I practiced rhyme, internal rhyme, and mimicked the movements of the Beats and the Lost Generation. I was an amateur — but I kept jabbing on paper.

Then one of those jabs landed. I won a poetry award from the Maryland State Poetry Society. They spelled my name wrong in the paper — *"BOOKMAN WINS POETRY AWARD"* — paid me $25 for the first rights to my poem.

A few months later, Loyola College selected me and a dozen others for a college poets' anthology and invited us to read on campus for a weekend.

And then I went quiet.

Poetry, I thought, would either call me again later in life... or become just a dream deferred — or what Eugene O'Neill called a *pipe dream* in *The Iceman Cometh*.

Years passed. My father's tavern, like the poetry section in bookstores, became a relic. With bankruptcy looming, I took a swing and turned it into a comedy club — one of only a few in existence at the time. Some said no one would come to Anacostia, especially when it was called the *"Murder Capital of the World."* Others said a comedy club was as unlikely as a poetry reading in a bar.

I sold into my obstacles.

The stage — actually, just a step — sat next to the front door. It wasn't ideal, but it trained our amateur comics. That door became their punching bag. They learned to jab at late arrivals and fight for control of the room. Eventually, it became a thing: show up late, get roasted by comics as the packed house roared.

Word of mouth spread. The phones rang nonstop. The directions were always the same, delivered in a line by comic Bill Thomas:

"After you pass the Capitol, follow Pennsylvania Ave over the Sousa Bridge, and when you really start to feel afraid, look to your left — that's where we are."

In the early days, I had trouble finding enough comics, so I stepped onto the stage myself. Hard to believe, but the first guy to answer my tiny ad in *The Washington Post* was Lewis Black — fresh out of the Yale School of Drama. The youngest performer was a twelve-year-old named Tom Rhodes, who showed up to watch his Uncle Bob perform. Tom got pulled onstage that night, heard the laughter, and knew he wanted to be a comic. He's one of the best working today.

Others went on to write for *Seinfeld*, *Roseanne*, and other classic shows. Some appeared in movies and on national stages. D.C.'s comedy roots are stronger — with Dave Chappelle leading the way.

That story — our story — was honored in Rich Shydner's book *Kicking Through the Ashes*, about the 1980s comedy boom. He wrote:

*"The place was crammed nightly. Med students from Georgetown. Midshipmen from Annapolis. Staffers from Capitol Hill. The draw was wide and the mix electric. Newly hired waitresses had to step over people in the aisles. Lines snaked down the sidewalk. Local kids were paid to watch the

parked BMWs, Mercedes-Benzes, and limos with embassy plates. The fire marshal looked at the jam-packed room, ordered the back door be kept unlocked, had a beer, and stayed for the show. Uniformed police officers spent their breaks watching the comedy, never checking identification or the funny cigarettes. Everyone was supportive of this miracle happening in Southeast."*

Lately, poetry has called me back. And I'm jabbing again.

The jab — the quiet, patient setup — is still the most important punch.

No matter how wild life swings at you, just keep jabbing.

And always — *get those hands up.*

Paul Brookman

elbrookman@outlook.com

Acknowledgments

*My brother and his wife Peggy for allowing me to escape to their fabulous beach house near Fenwick Island whenever I needed to get out of Annapolis this past summer.

*My brother John, who didn't declare my insanity when shown a mock up cover for the book but said he would buy it. I knew then, (John is a little stingy with a dollar,) I had to complete it.

*My cousin Pat. She has always been supportive of my creative endeavors.

*My Amazing and creative friend Angie, the Georgia Casserole Queen. Thank you, and glad I'm not around to eat your famous hot dog casserole.